The Gods Must Be Angry

A true story from Thailand

For Edyth and Selene
with appreciation and love

Published by OMF International
10 West Dry Creek Circle, Littleton CO 80120

ISBN: 9971-972-93-X

First published 1990
Second printing 2004
This printing 2012

Printed in the United States of America.

OMF Books are distributed worldwide.
Visit *www.OMFBooks.com* for more information.

"Here comes the band!" called Somsak.

Bradit peered round the head of the boy in front. He'd never seen a band in all his life.

But one was coming. Right now. He could hear the music. Tir-rum-pa-pum. Tir-rum-pa-pum, pum, pum ... All the school kids on the playing field were high with excitement.

The senior students appeared at the starting line. There at the head was the band major. All in white. Dressed up for the band with a red sash over one shoulder.

Bradit saw him striding ahead of the others, a flat hat like a hamburger carton on his head. And then Bradit saw the pole in his right hand. The band major waved the pole with its white, blue and red streamers. White, blue and red for Thailand.

The band major swung the pole. He twirled the pole. The streamers flew out behind him like bright butterflies. They fluttered even though there was no wind and the sun was so hot.

"Left wheel," shouted the band major. Out went the big pole to the left while the trumpeters, drummers and pipers turned. Tir-rum-pa-pum. Deedle-deedle-dum. Wow! The tall pole with the streamers worked like magic! Bradit had never heard or seen anything so fantastic.

He stamped his feet on the caked soil just like the band major. "Left wheel!" he yelled, just like the band major. He swung his arms in the air.

"Hey, hey, hey! You watch it! That was my ear!" roared Somsak.

But Bradit didn't hear his cousin. Sports' Day at Somsak's school was cool. Track events, jumping, team games, ball games, everything all in one day. And then a *band*! The band was the best!

The musicians' shadows grew long in the evening sun. It was time for them to march home. Bradit marched behind them along the road until it forked. He took the left lane then, because it was nearly dark. In Thailand night time falls fast when the sun sets.

Thailand is a country miles and miles away, in the tropical part of the world where it's very hot; not far from the equator. A land of wooden houses built on stilts and big colored temples; a land of sticky rice and mangoes; of jungle and palm trees; elephants and Siamese cats. It would take you a whole day to get there in a jumbo jet.

It's a land of bamboo. Bamboo is a special sort of cane which grows in Thailand in a tall bush, like poles with feathery leaves. Bradit took the

left lane to his bamboo house built high off the ground on its four long wooden legs. Just a little way down the lane stood a temple. A Buddhist temple. The religion of almost all the Thai people is Buddhism.

Bradit's heart began to thump like a jack-hammer. There in the temple grounds were more drummers. These drummers were not making marching music. Instead the drums banged and thumped. Bradit knew why. Somebody in the village had died. The drummers were scaring

away any bad spirits that might be around during the funeral.

Even in the warm dusky air, Bradit felt a chill creep through him. The spirit of the dead person was floating about. It mustn't see him. He fled towards home as fast as the runner of the 100-meter race at his cousin's school. But he wasn't thinking of the Sports' Day any longer. He'd even forgotten for the moment about the band. He just wanted to get home, away from that fierce floating spirit.

Twelve hours later, morning spread its light through the village. Bradit stretched on his mat. It was Saturday! No school! Great! And then all the fun of yesterday flooded his memory just like the early sunlight dancing on the tallest tree tops.

"Bradit!" called Mom.

"Mm-m?" answered Bradit. He hoped his mother didn't want him to do the shopping. Bradit didn't want to go to market. His mind was full of Somsak's school band. Today he could play band! The music from the game played in his head like a grand march. He could …

"Bradit!"

"Yes, Mom?"

"I need to buy sugar so I'll take some chickens to sell at the market. I'll go on the bus with Yupa.

Look after the house and be a good boy while I'm gone."

The bus! That meant the *far-away* market. Mom wouldn't be back till the afternoon! Bradit beamed. That would mean all morning to play!

"Are you listening, Bradit?"

"Mm … Yes. Bye Mom."

Today Bradit didn't care about missing the bus ride. Even with the bus windows open it would be so hot. Bradit didn't feel like being crushed into a hot bus. Not with all the baskets of fruit and vegetables. Not on top of all those squawking chickens. Not today anyway.

Bradit jumped up from his mat and waved. He waved and hummed. Tir-um-tum-tum. Tir-um-tum-tum. Underneath the house his chickens scratched around looking for any leftover seeds from last night's supper. Bradit's brown dog, Brownie, was there too. He'd found shady place for a morning nap. The music drummed louder and louder in Bradit's head. Standing in the doorway he could almost see the school band marching by.

"Tiddle-ump-pum-pum," sang Bradit to the empty house. What a neat day yesterday had been. Out in the field in the sun. No math. No staring at the Thai alphabet with all its squiggles.

No
anything
but races and a
band. Tir-a-um-pum. Tir-
a-um-pum.

Mom and Yupa were now out of sight. Bradit skipped away from the open door with the music in his head still beating out a fine rhythm. He whistled his way across the room. The house didn't have much furniture under its leafy roof. Just a chair and a table in one corner. The most important thing in the house was called the idol shelf. The idol shelf was red and shiny gold. It had the best place — high up on the bamboo wall.

Bradit's family knew nothing about the real God — the God who made Thailand; the God who made *them*. They didn't know anything either about God's Son, the Lord Jesus.

So when they said their prayers they prayed to idols which sat high on the idol shelf. Up there were some pictures, incense sticks which made a sweet smell when they were burning, and little saucers of food. Every night Bradit's mother prayed there and on special days she would light the incense sticks and put saucers of food in front of the idols as an offering.

Two idols sat on the idol shelf. One was tall and thin, standing straight and serious. This was the Sad Idol. The other was short and very fat. It sat cross-legged with a big smile. This was the Happy Idol.

"Tum, tum, ti-tum, ti-tum, deedle, deedle, dum ti-tum," sang Bradit loudly to no one in particular because there was nobody there. He went on humming between mouthfuls of breakfast rice. Then his eyes suddenly saw a big stick lying in the corner. Bradit picked it up. He could be the leader —the leader of the school band, marching up and down the playing field in a great ceremony.

The house shook as he stamped on the bamboo floor. Swish, swish. He waved the stick through the air. Swish, swish. He was conducting the music. Tum, tum, ti-tum, ti-tum. Deedle, deedle, dum-ti-tum.

March, march and deedle, deedle dum.

Left, left and left, right left.

Shake, shake and swish, swish, swish.

Swish, swish and shake, shake, shake.

Thud.

Oh *no* …

Bradit's conducting stick had swung out farther than he'd meant it to. Oh *no* — just a little bit too far. And he'd been too close to the idol shelf. The long stick had struck one of the idols.

The head of the Happy Idol lay at Bradit's feet.

Bradit's playtime was ruined. This was a terrible disaster. The idol was a sacred object of worship in their family. Bad luck would come to them all now. Yes, an accident like this would bring them very bad luck. The fierce floating spirit of the dead person could find him and the gods would pay him back for breaking the Happy Idol.

And what in the wide world was Dad going to

say when he found out? Bradit swallowed hard in a great gulp. His father would soon be home from the paddy fields where his rice was growing, for a rest from the super-hot sun in the middle of the day. What on earth was he to do.

His heart was thumping away inside him. In a panic Bradit grabbed the three-legged stool. He dragged it over to the idol shelf. Then carefully, very carefully, he picked up the head of the Happy Idol. Standing on the seat he could just reach the shelf. Carefully, very carefully, he balanced the head on top of the idol's shoulders. There is sat looking *almost* right. Hardly daring to breathe, Bradit slipped off the stool, tiptoed across the floor, hid his conducting stick behind the table and sat down miserably in the corner to wait.

He sat there wishing he'd gone to market. He sat there wishing he'd never found the long stick. He could have been a trumpeter. He could have clenched his fists up to his mouth and tooted the music through his hands. Why did he ever decide to lead the band? It was no good now being a trumpeter. He didn't want to play band anymore … He didn't want to play band ever again …

He thought of climbing down the ladder to sit with Brownie under the house where the air was

cooler but — that might make the floor shake again. That might make the head of the Happy Idol wobble.

Under the house next door, the neighbors were hammering at an old buffalo cart. Bradit sat there miserably listening to the bang, bang, bang of the hammer, listening to the Thai voices, listening to

… oh help! Now he could hear another sound — Father kicking off his thongs at the bottom of the ladder.

The water in the basin splashed as Dad washed the mud off the paddy fields from his legs. And then clomp, clomp, clomp, he climbed the ladder.

The house shook — just a little.

Dad came in. "Hallo there, Bradit. What are you doing?"

"Nothing, Dad."

"I forgot my stick this morning. I should always have it in case I find a snake in the paddy. Did you see it?"

"No, Dad."

Bradit's father walked across the bamboo floor. The house shook a little bit more.

He moved closer to the idol shelf where the idols were sitting much as before — the thin Sad Idol and the fat Happy Idol. He never even glanced up at them.

As he got nearer, the room shook just that little bit more.

And then …

The head of the Happy Idol toppled off with a dull thump on the floor.

Father stopped. He stood very still. Horrified, he gazed at the grinning face of the Happy Idol down there on the floor near his feet.

"Who did this?" he roared.

Bradit sat shaking and quaking in his corner. He couldn't answer. He never said a word.

Dad examined the broken idol.

"This head has been knocked off recently," he thundered. "It didn't happen all by itself!"

He turned and stared at Bradit.

"Bradit! Did you do this?"

"N-n-no, Daddy," stammered Bradit.

Just outside, their neighbor's hammer banged at the broken buffalo cart.

"Hi!" called Bradit's father. "Has anyone been up in this house? Did you hear anyone making a noise up here?"

"No," called Mr Next-door Neighbor. "Nobody has been in the house since you left. Only your son. Bradit was having a great time, marching around and swinging a stick as if he were the school band major!"

Bradit's father grabbed him by the ear.

"So it *was* you," he hissed. "You did it! You broke the head of the Happy Idol!"

"No. No Daddy ..."

"This is terrible," roared Dad. "It will bring all kinds of bad luck. The household gods will be furious ..."

"Daddy, Daddy, it wasn't me," cried Bradit. "It was the Sad Idol who did it. The Sad Idol hates the Happy Idol because he's always laughing at him. So he just knocked his head off."

"Ha! Impossible!" yelled Bradit's father. "The Sad Idol never did that! Idols can't possibly do that sort of thing!"

Bradit sobbed, "Daddy, if the idols can't do that to one another how can they help us?"

Dad had no reply. He was still very angry. He

found his stick for killing snakes behind the table. And he spanked Bradit for such a terrible thing. For knocking the head off the Happy Idol.

How come, though, the Sad Idol couldn't fix him?

How come the Happy Idol couldn't fix himself?

With his face all swollen with crying, Bradit watched his father set off for the rice fields again. Bradit's father was swinging the stick for killing snakes. *I wish he hadn't forgotten it this morning,* thought Bradit, tenderly feeling his bruises.

Rice likes to grow in water. Father's paddy field was flooded with water, oozy coffee-colored water because of the mud underneath. Bradit's father rolled up his baggy trousers to his knees, kicked off his thongs and waded into the brown lake which was really his rice field.

One by one he took the small rice plants and set them to grow in the mud under the water. Bending and planting. Planting and bending. The sun's beams burned on his back. Bradit's father felt hot and tired. Besides, he kept thinking of the broken Happy Idol.

He wished he could stop thinking about it. Bradit, Bradit, why did you do it? When would the bad luck start? Why did the idol break if it

was a real god? Why couldn't the Happy Idol fix himself? Why? Why? All the "whys" went round and round in father's head like a bongo drum beating time. Why — why — why?

And at home, during the hot afternoon, Bradit's mother arrived back with Yupa from the market. She saw Bradit under the house with his arm round his big brown dog. Then she climbed the ladder and saw something else. She saw the Happy Idol sitting on the idol shelf with hits head sitting beside it!

"Oh, I don't believe it!" she gasped.

"Bradit! What's this? What has happened?" Her brown cheeks paled with fright.

"Bradit! What's this I see?" she called again.

Bradit knew by the tone of her voice that he'd better run — but with amazing speed his mother leaped down the ladder before he could make a getaway. She caught him by the shoulders. She shook him. She shook him till the whole explanation spilled out.

Bradit's mother was horrified.

"Now I shall have to buy a new idol," she wailed. "I'll have to get one before the bad luck

starts. The fierce spirit of the Happy Idol will come looking for revenge. I'll have to go to the temple and get the monk to bless another household god. This will cost a lot of money. Oh I just can't believe it ..."

Bradit's mother dragged him up the ladder. She shook him again and stood there shaking with fear herself. Yupa clung to her mother's skirt, not understanding a thing. She decided to scream anyway because of the hubbub around her.

But it was time to cook the rice for supper and very soon Bradit heard his father coming home from the paddy fields. He heard his voice calling to the next door neighbor, "Got the buffalo cart fixed, then?"

"No. Can't do it!"

"Take it to the old cart maker in the next village," called Father. "He was the one who made it, so he is the best one to fix it for you."

Then Father sloshed water all over his muddy feet and climbed the ladder.

Father felt better after he had washed. The cool water from the tank was refreshing. He used a dipper pan to throw the water all over him. The water from the dipper trickled down over his shoulders, showering the floor with puddles which soaked right through the bamboo down to the chickens below waiting for their supper. Soon he was dressed in a clean shirt, his wet black hair all shiny.

"I'll walk across to Brasong's house," he said to Mother after eating. "I'll borrow his saw. I think it would be good to make a new idol shelf. That should please the spirits."

Bradit watched his father walk away in the evening light. He wondered if his father was scared to pass the temple at the end of the lane. He wondered if the dead person's fierce floating spirit had found somewhere to go. *I wish there were no such things as spirits,* thought Bradit to himself. *I'm always afraid of them. Are they really floating round in the air? Do we always have to do things to please them?*

It seemed to take just about forever before Bradit's father arrived home in the dark with Brasong's saw.

"What kept you?" asked Bradit's mom, looking up from her straight-line embroidery which she could just about see to do in the light of a kerosene lamp.

"Yes, well, we had some sticky rice cakes to eat together and sweet red juice to drink," explained Bradit's father. "And there I was enjoying the

food when I noticed a very strange thing ..." He paused, then added, "Brasong's idol shelf had disappeared!"

"Is he having bad luck?" asked Bradit's mother fearfully. She crept back into the shadows of the room and leaned on the bamboo wall.

"I don't think so. Not so far anyway."

"Is he making a new shelf?"

"No. That's just it. Brasong and his wife threw away their idol shelf purposely."

Bradit's eyes widened. What would the spirits do to Brasong for that terrible thing?

"Yes," said Bradit's father. "They've taken the shelf down and everything to do with it."

"Why?" whispered his mother. She was afraid the bad spirits would hear.

"Well, Brasong's cousin in the next village has become a Christian. And he lent Brasong a book to read. A book called the Bible. In there it tells you that God made the world. Brasong says He is the true, real God — He's the one who made us too. I didn't know that before."

Bradit never knew that before either. He crept into the shadows too. He didn't want his father to notice he hadn't gone to his sleeping mat yet. He wanted to stay up just a bit longer and hear what happened.

"In this Bible," his father was saying, "it tells you about God's Son. He is called the Lord Jesus. It tells you about how He died and then came back to life."

"Did Brasong tell you *that*?" exclaimed Bradit's mother. "That's impossible!"

"Well, Brasong says Jesus is alive. Brasong says he and his wife have asked this Jesus to be in charge of them for the rest of their lives."

Bradit nearly started into a whole line of

questions but he remembered just in time that he wasn't meant to be there. Why did Jesus die? Was He killed? If He came to life again He must be a God. How could you know if this story was true?

"We Thai people," his father was saying, "we try to get to heaven by doing good things but," he paused, frowning, "but doing good things doesn't cover up our bad things. Brasong says we ought to be *punished* for sins."

You bet! thought Bradit, feeling his bruises in the darkness.

"But, you see," his father was still talking, "if Jesus took the blame, then we don't need to be punished! Then we don't need to work our way to heaven after all!"

The little bamboo house on stilts was strangely quiet for a time. Then Bradit heard his father whisper, a note of excitement creeping into his voice. "Jesus took the blame. He died instead of me! You know, we could be forgiven too! Like Brasong. Like his wife. Like his cousin Narin ..."

And that night Bradit's father did not make a new idol shelf after all.

Not that night, nor the next, nor the next ...

"I'll just walk over to Brasong's house again," he called to Bradit's mother, a week later.

This time Bradit busied himself in a corner

well within earshot. He wanted to still be there when his father came back. He wanted to hear if his father knew any more things about the Christian's Bible. What did it say in there about floating spirits? Was this true God stronger than the fierce spirits?

His eyes had begun to close with drowsiness by the time his father climbed the ladder again. But then, suddenly, he was awake. Wide awake.

"Is Brasong okay?" his mother was calling. "Have the spirits attacked him? Is he sick? Is the fruit still growing on his trees? His papayas? His mangoes? His lamyai ...?"

"Wait, wait," Bradit's father said. "He's fine. His new God is stronger than all the spirits. Nothing's wrong."

"What if his family gets ill?"

"Brasong says if our cart breaks down, the cart maker is the best one to fix it. So if something does go wrong His new God will protect him and help him."

Bradit's mother broke into sobs. "I'm afraid of the spirit of the broken idol," she whispered.

"So am I," wailed Bradit, entirely forgetting that he should be asleep on his mat, "and I'm afraid of the spirit of the dead person."

"What dead person? Wait. Let's think this thing out," Bradit's Dad said. "Idols by themselves can't have any power. After all they're just made by people. Old Uncle Dee in the next village — he made that Happy Idol years ago. The Sad Idol couldn't fix him. They can't help each other so they can't help us. At least that's what Brasong said.

"I've always been afraid of the fierce spirits of the idols too," he went on. "But Brasong says his new God is more powerful than all the spirits."

And then they sat down on the floor together and nobody said anything at all.

Bradit's father was thinking, *Should we take the*

idol shelf down then? I would need to ask Brasong how to pray to the true God instead.

Bradit's mother was thinking, *That fat idol has no head on it now. But what difference has that made to our lives?*

Bradit was thinking, *Don't we need to be afraid of floating spirits after all?*

As they went off to bed at last, Bradit's father's arm was around Bradit's shoulders.

One day, not very long after this, Bradit arrived home from school to see a strange sight. His father was climbing down their ladder with heavy deliberate steps. In his arms was a big cardboard box. He looked like a removal man carrying furniture to a truck. Only there was no truck in the garden. But in the garden, was a small crowd of people! They watched as the big cardboard box came nearer.

Inside the box was the family idol shelf. Inside the box was the Sad Idol and the Happy Idol with its head broken off. In there were the incense sticks from the idol shelf, the pictures and the little saucers for food. Bradit's father had brought the whole thing down.

Bradit dumped his writing and reading books in the house and jumped down into the garden with a great big leap. He felt as if he could fly through the air, he was so excited. What was Dad going to do? A small chill of fear crept down his spine. Was it a good thing to take away their idol shelf?

Then he noticed Mr Brasong and his wife. He saw Mr Narin and other people he didn't know from the next village. Yupa was running round in a circle beside her mother, and Brownie, his big dog, was coming to see what in the world was going on.

The Christian people began to pray. They prayed to the real God. Then Bradit's father and mother prayed too. They said, "Lord Jesus, we want to worship you only. Forgive us for all the wrong things we have ever done. Come into our lives and help us to live for you. Protect us from the fierce spirits." Then they started to sing, happily, loudly, enjoying every word.

A Thai farmer gave Bradit's father a book. "Here are the teachings of Jesus for you," he said.

And Bradit's dad said to Bradit. "Here Bradit, you hold the book. I have something I want to do."

Bradit held the book with great care. He wanted to look at it even though his reading wasn't very good yet. But he couldn't just then because he was watching his father. Out of his

pocket, Bradit's father took a box of matches.

Dad lit five matches. And the five matches kindled the flames around all of the idol shelf, the Sad Idol, the headless Happy Idol and everything in the cardboard box. Everything was burned up in Bradit's garden, with the Christians all watching. And then they began to sing again …

Bradit peered through the fire and saw his dad's smiling face. Then he looked again and saw his mom's smiling face. It seemed as though they were glowing; glowing just like the flames. I'm going to be a Christian, too, thought Bradit.

His father moved across to him. "Bradit," he whispered, "do you know why this has happened? It's because you broke the Happy Idol! You thought it was a mistake but see — it has made us like new people!"

A big, big smile like a slice of watermelon lit up Bradit's face too. He stood in the garden with his dad on one side and Brownie on the other. He stood there wondering — wondering if there were bands in heaven.

Today Bradit is a father himself and the pastor of a church in Thailand, where he is teaching about the Lord Jesus, the true God who made all things. This story is based on the testimony of Bradit (not his real name) as told to Ian Murray.